MAISIE'S FESTIVAL ADVENTURE

Author and Illustrator: Aileen Paterson

This story is dedicated to my friends Jane Soeder and Davena Turvey.
With thanks to Liz and Adam Wight

© Aileen Paterson

Published in 1988 by
The Amaising Publishing House Ltd.
P.O. Box
Musselburgh
EH21 7UJ
Scotland

031-665 8237

Reprinted 1992
Printed & Bound by Scotprint Ltd, Musselburgh

ISBN 1 871512 04 2

Other Maisie Titles in the Series:

Maisie goes to School

Maisie and the Posties

Maisie goes to Hospital

Maisie loves Paris

Maisie and the Space Invader

What Maisie did Next

Maisie in the Rainforest

It was Festival time in Edinburgh. The streets were crowded with tourists, the weather was crisp and sunny, and there was so much to do and see.

Early one morning, the clip-clopping of a horse's hooves could be heard in Granny's street. Maisie looked out of the window.

"There's Tommy the milk cat now, Granny," she cried.

"Run down and tell him we'll be needing two extra pints every day this week, Maisie," said Granny, "and tell him I've put the kettle on!"

Maisie took some sugar lumps out of the bowl and ran down-stairs. She gave Tommy the message, and then she went over to Hamish, his friendly old horse, patted him, and fed him the sugar.

Hamish, the last milk-horse in Edinburgh, was greatly loved by everyone on his round.

Tommy tied a bag of oats on Hamish for his breakfast, then Maisie helped him to deliver the milk in the stair before they went into Granny's kitchen.

Granny poured out the tea, and sat down to enjoy a blether with Tommy, but the news he had to tell her that day was sad. The Dairy had decided to buy an electric milk float, and send Hamish away to live in the country.

Tommy was very upset.

"I'm going to miss him after all these years," he said. "He's grand company, and as strong as a Horse! I can't have a conversation with a wee van. Och, it's the end of civilisation as we know it, Mrs MacKenzie."

Granny shook her head, sadly. She didn't like changes, at her age, she said, and Hamish was like a friend.

Maisie looked out of the window, the old horse would be sadly missed.

Granny changed the subject to try and cheer everyone up.

She told Tommy all about her visitors. They were Mounted Police, and they'd come all the way from Canada to appear at the Tattoo up at the Castle.

Suddenly, the kitchen door swept open. It was Mrs McKitty from next door, looking very excited.

"I've got the most wonderful news for you, Isabella," she cried, "My cousin Griselda, the famous Opera Star, arrived last night. She's giving a recital this morning at the Usher Hall and as a special treat, she's invited you all in to hear her sing. She says it will help to warm up her voice!"

Tommy, who was not an opera-lover, thanked Mrs McKitty, but said he had to get on with his milk round.

Granny and Maisie followed Mrs McKitty into her parlour, to be introduced.

Madame Griselda, as she was known, was a very large cat. To give them all the flavour of her song (about warriors charging into battle) she was carrying a shield and a spear, and on her head was a helmet with horns sticking out!

Granny and Maisie couldn't believe their eyes.

Madame Griselda bowed to everyone, cleared her throat, then launched forth. Her voice, rich and powerful, filled the room. The windows rattled! The ceiling shook! Neighbours knocked! Maisie put her paws over her ears. As the song ended—on a high C— disaster struck.

All the crystal glasses in Mrs McKitty's display cabinet exploded, one after another.

Billy the budgie, who had been singing along with the Opera Star, fell to the bottom of his cage and waved his legs in the air!

It had been too much for him.

No one clapped.

Madame Griselda was furious. She swept out and left for the theatre!

Granny began sweeping up the glass, while Maisie rushed over and revived the budgie with a splash of water.

Mrs McKitty sat down looking dazed.

Granny made her a cup of tea and put a cold compress on her head.

Back in their flat, Granny began preparing breakfast for the Mounties.

"Thank goodness our visitors are nice quiet bodies," she said to Maisie, then she began to laugh. "If that's Opera, then give me a nice Pipe Band, anytime."

Maisie set the table, then in came Mike and Bob, the two Mounties.

She fetched their porridge, but when they asked for sugar to sprinkle on it, she said "Granny doesn't allow sugar on porridge. Scottish cats take it with a little salt and some cream from the top of the milk." They laughed and agreed to try it Granny's way, and said they liked it.

While they ate their Ayrshire bacon, buttery rolls, and fried eggs with lacy brown edges, Maisie asked them about Canada and their work.

"What is a Mountie?" she asked.

"Well, Maisie," said Mike, "we are Policecats, just like you have here in Scotland, but we chase robbers mounted on our horses. That's how we got our name."

"Canada has lots of wild places," Bob told her, "Sometimes we trail a thief for days, through forests, over mountains, across rivers—even in deep snow. But we never give up. Mounties always catch them in the end."

He fetched his uniform and Maisie tried it on. It was far too big for her and the hat came down over her eyes but her imagination worked wonders. She could just see herself galloping along on the trail of some wicked desperado.

Maisie, the fearless Mountie!

Granny's voice brought her down to earth again.

"Maisie," she called, "Bob and Mike would like to explore Edinburgh this morning and I said you could be their guide if you like."

Maisie said she would be delighted to show them the city.

They wanted to buy some presents to take home, so she took them to a shop where they bought lovely Scottish jerseys and scarves, then on to a sweetie shop, where they bought Edinburgh Rock for their own wee kittens.

The Mounties were very impressed with historic old Edinburgh, and very proud of their Scottish ancestors.

They explored the Castle with Maisie and took photographs of her in her kilt, sitting on top of one of the old cannons.

She led them down into Princes Street to watch all the entertainers. There were acrobats, jugglers, musicians and pavement artists, even a one-cat band. He played the banjo while he blew on a mouth organ, his elbows banged a drum and his knees clashed a pair of cymbals!

Maisie sat down to watch a Punch and Judy show. There were kittens there from all over the world, cheering at Mr Punch's antics. Bob and Mike roared with laughter when Punch knocked the Policecat's helmet off, and shouted, "That's the way to do it!"

When the show ended, they strolled into Princes Street Gardens and watched the cuckoo pop out of the Floral Clock on the hour.

They had lunch at the Sit-Ooterie Cafe and enjoyed sitting in the Autumn sunshine.

Maisie organised a game of Hunt-the-Haggis, and Mike and Bob really believed her story—that the Haggis is a wee grey animal that feeds on thistles and neeps, and is found only in Scotland—until the Haggis they were stalking ran out of the bushes, and turned out to be nothing more than a grey squirrel!

(After that they chased Maisie!)

She decided to round off their tour of Edinburgh with a visit to Holyrood Palace, so they climbed the hill again, and joined a pipe band marching down the Royal Mile. Maisie strode out in front beside the Pipe-Major, waggling her kilt in time to the skirl of the music, while Bob and Mike took photographs from the pavement.

Through the palace gates they marched, and when they stopped at the front door, Maisie skipped back to her friends.

They joined a party of tourists being shown round by a guide. As soon as they went inside the old Palace, they could feel its atmosphere of romance and mystery. They followed the guide up the narrow winding stair.

What a tale of murder and mayhem he unfolded, as he told them the tragic history of Mary, Queen of Cats.

"This is the very spot where her secretary was done to death," he announced gloomily, pointing to the floor. "His ghost can sometimes be heard, playing a violin."

Maisie shivered, and took hold of Mike's paw.

They crowded into a small room at the top of the stairs, and gathered in front of a portrait of the beautiful Queen. Not a sound could be heard. Everyone was entranced.

Suddenly the eerie silence was broken by loud squeals from the crowd. Maisie jumped with alarm!

"Help! my purse has been stolen! Stop that thief! My wallet! My camera!"

And from the shadows dashed a sly-looking, fast-moving grey cat. He dived out of the little door, and down the stairs, but when the others tried to follow they all got jammed in the narrow corridor.

Luckily for Maisie, she was wee, and able to squeeze past all the legs and tails and paws, and wriggle her way out.

She flew after him and ran out into the grounds.

There he was, rushing out of the gates! My, he was quick, but Maisie was determined to keep on his trail, and catch him, just like a Mountie.

He turned, saw her in hot pursuit and, to her dismay, she saw him hail a passing taxi and jump in.

Thinking she had lost her chance, Maisie almost burst into tears!

But help was at hand, for just at that moment, she heard the clip-clopping of a horse's hooves, and there was Hamish trotting past on his way to the stables, with Tommy holding the reins.

Maisie's hopes rose again!

"Hamish," she cried. "Help! Stop!"

The old horse reared to a halt by the pavement, and Maisie clambered on to his back.

"Quick," she shouted. "FOLLOW THAT TAXI. There's a thief inside, and we've got to stop him."

Hamish pricked his ears back, and set off at a gallop after the taxi, his hooves striking sparks on the cobblestones as they thundered on. Maisie clung firmly to his mane, while Tommy clutched grimly at the reins, and tried to come to grips with what was happening.

One minute he and Hamish had been going quietly home to their stable, and now they were on this amazing chase through the streets of Edinburgh!

They followed the speeding taxi into the busy traffic of deepest Tollcross, then suddenly, when it halted at traffic lights, the robber jumped out and ran off.

Maisie knew it was NOW or NEVER!

Tommy was horrified to see her stand up on Hamish's back as they drew alongside the robber. When she was right above him— she JUMPED!

There was a terrific thump as she landed, flattening the thief on the pavement.

By the time Tommy had halted Hamish and jumped down, Maisie was sitting on top of her struggling captive.

Soon they were joined by the taxi-driver and two policecats.

"Well done, young kitten," they said, putting the pawcuffs on their puffed-out prisoner.

"This is Quick-Paw McGraw, the international pick-pocket. We've been after him for years."

"He owes me my fare too!" cried the taxi-driver.

Bob and Mike came running up just in time to see Maisie's moment of triumph. She told them about the chase as Tommy drove them home in the milk-cart . . .

Granny and Mrs McKitty were astounded by the tale of Maisie's Festival adventure, but very pleased that she was safe, and that all had ended well.

As a reward, the policecats gave her a night out at the Festival with all her friends.

First they had a fine sea-food dinner in Leith, where they were entertained by a trio playing piano, flute and violin; then they were given a box at the theatre to see a Ballet called "Sleeping Sooty."

"Pay attention, little kittens," said Mrs McKitty, "This is a night to remember—I've always loved the Ballet, you know."

The little kittens were very amused when she fell asleep, half-way through!

They enjoyed every minute of it.

After the Ballet, they were driven up to the Castle for the Tattoo. Their seats were perched high above the Castle Esplanade. The sky was nearly black, and Granny tucked rugs round everyone, for the night wind whistled round their paws and whiskers.

Down below, everything was brilliantly lit up, and the marching soldiers played marvellous music. "This is just my cup of tea," said Granny.

She loved the pipes!

The last part of the show began with the Canadian Mounties, on their beautiful horses, leading a grand parade.

Suddenly the music stopped, and a voice over the loudspeakers asked for Miss Maisie MacKenzie to come down and join them.

Rather nervously, she stepped into the limelight and, in front of the huge audience, she was presented with a little Mountie jacket and hat.

Then out of the darkness trotted Hamish the milk–horse, all brushed and groomed and saddled.

The announcer told everyone about Maisie following the trail of the thief, and how Hamish had helped her.

They cheered and clapped!

Mike and Bob lifted her into the saddle; then she and Hamish led the Mounties twice round the Esplanade, while the bands played.

It was a magical evening, and a great adventure!
When they got home they watched the Festival fireworks lighting up the Edinburgh sky.

Granny made cocoa for everyone, then Tommy the milk-cat stood up.

"Just before I go home," he said to Granny and Maisie, "I want to thank you all for a grand evening, and to tell you my good news. The Dairy have decided to keep Hamish. With all the publicity about catching the thief, and being a star at the Festival, they've changed their minds about his being too old. Besides, he'll be a wonderful advertisement for their milk!"

Maisie was overjoyed. What a happy ending!

When she went to bed, very late, that night, Granny tucked her in and said, "My word, Maisie, I never thought the Festival could be such a treat, but I've had the night of my life. Next year I'll book tickets for everything!"

"Even the Opera?" asked Maisie with a smile.
"We'll see, said Granny, smiling, too.
And then she kissed her Good-Night.

Glossary:

blether	chat
neeps	turnips, swedes
Sit-Ooterie	patio